To all who are waiting, unknowingly, to be free.

Thanks to Radiohead for "Bloom", which provided deep inspiration as I wrote;
to Rebecca, who turned somersaults with me; and to Anne Schwartz,
who knew the song that Wednesday sang – T.H.
For Mum – R.J.

PUFFIN BOOKS

UK | USA | Canada | Ireland | Australia
India | New Zealand | South Africa

Puffin Books is part of the Penguin Random House group of companies
whose addresses can be found at global.penguinrandomhouse.com.

www.penguin.co.uk
www.puffin.co.uk
www.ladybird.co.uk

First published in the United States of America by Schwartz & Wade Books,
an imprint of Random House Children's Books, a division of Penguin Random House LLC, 2018
Published in Great Britain by Puffin Books 2020

001

Text copyright © Troy Howell, 2018
Illustrations copyright © Richard Jones, 2018

The moral right of the author and illustrator has been asserted

Printed in China

A CIP catalogue record for this book is available from the British Library

ISBN: 978–0–241–41881–9

All correspondence to:
Puffin Books, Penguin Random House Children's
One Embassy Gardens, 8 Viaduct Gardens, London SW11 7BW

Whale in a Fishbowl

Troy Howell & Richard Jones

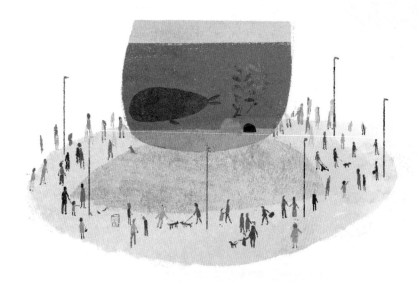

PUFFIN

Wednesday lived in a fishbowl.
It was the only home she knew.

Her name was Wednesday because, like the day of the week,
she was smack in the middle of everything.

Everything circled around her.

People – flurrying, hurrying, worrying.

Traffic – wheeling, pealing, squealing.

Even the sun, moon and stars circled around her.
Everything . . .

. . . but a calm bit of blue that lay at the end of it all.

It was there if she leaped high enough.

Her heart leaped, too, when she saw it, though she didn't know why.

Mostly, she would drift, watching the world go by.

People and cars,
day and night.

Then she'd think about the
blue and wish to see it again.

She'd gather her strength and make the leap.
There the blue lay, beautiful.

Soon she couldn't get enough of the blue.

People said she was doing tricks.

"Ah!" they said. "Look!"

Crowds clapped. Horns honked.

Wednesday would leap and leap.

Leaping became her routine.

But sometimes she'd lie along the bottom.
She'd try burying her head in the sand.

One morning a girl in a paisley dress approached
and tapped on the glass.
Wednesday came close.
"Hey," the girl said.

Wednesday gazed into her eyes. She had seen that blue before.

"I'm Piper," said the girl. "And you're lovely."

Wednesday's reflection shone in Piper's eyes.

"But you don't belong in there."

Wednesday blinked.
She looked at her familiar shells and plants, at the starfish on the rock.
This was her home. If she didn't belong here, then where?

Piper was leaving – a woman was rushing her off.
But before they were lost in the crowd Piper called,
"You belong in the sea!"

The sea . . .

The sea . . .

What was the sea?

Wednesday wondered about it all day long, and all night, too.

What did the sea have that her fishbowl didn't have?

Now she couldn't sleep.

She scarcely touched her food.

She no longer leaped.

Could Piper have been wrong?

Piper wasn't a whale. What did a little girl know?

Without answers, Wednesday gave up on the sea.

And when she did she thought of the blue again.

She ached to see it.

So she gathered her strength, thrust her tail, and leaped.

The blue wasn't there.
Gone.
Nothing.
Nothing but grey.

Wednesday sank into the sand. Her heart hurt.
If she cried, her tears were lost to the water.

Then she lifted her head.
Maybe she hadn't leaped high enough.
She would try one final time.
If the blue wasn't there,
she would leap no more.

Up, up Wednesday leaped, higher than ever before.

So high, she leaped beyond the bowl.

Her tail caught the rim and the bowl toppled over.

Torrents of water gushed out.

The water carried Wednesday down the avenue,

past all she'd ever known.

It carried her into the grey.

But the grey was disappearing, giving way to something else.

A glorious, breathtaking blue. A blue that went on forever.

She plunged into it.
She swam and swam and swam.
She skimmed and soared,
spouted and dived.
She turned somersaults.
She swam strong and far and deep.

And for the first time in her life, she sang.

She sang about the blue and everything new around her.

She sang about Piper, who had known

where Wednesday belonged.

Here she was, at last.

Then there came someone just like her, who said,

"Hello. Welcome to the middle of the sea."